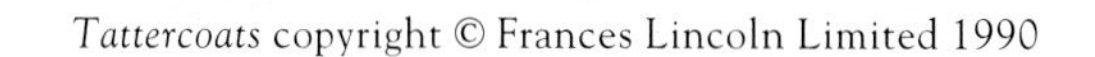

First published in Great Britain in 1990 by
Frances Lincoln Limited, 4 Torriano Mews
Torriano Avenue, London NW5 2RZ

First paperback edition 1995

British Library Cataloguing in Publication Data
available on request

ISBN 0-7112-0640-6 hardback
ISBN 0-7112-0649-X paperback

Set in Goudy Old Style by Goodfellow & Egan
Printed in Hong Kong

3 5 7 9 8 6 4 2

Tattercoats

retold by
Margaret Greaves

illustrated by
Margaret Chamberlain

FRANCES LINCOLN

There was once a girl who lived in an old, cold, grey castle with her old, cold, grey grandfather. Her parents had died when she was very young, and her grandfather disliked her. She reminded him too sadly of her mother, his favourite child. He was angry with her youth and beauty, for they made the castle seem even more gloomy by contrast.

So the poor girl was banished from his sight into the kitchen. He would give her neither food nor clothes. She lived on what scraps she could beg, and was dressed in cast-off rags and tatters. She was so thin and ragged and neglected that even the poorest servants laughed at her and called her Tattercoats. She could remember no other name.

Her grandfather sulked alone in the great rooms of his castle, until cobwebs covered the windows and moths ate holes in his velvet cloak and his beard grew almost to his feet.

But in spite of cold and hunger Tattercoats tried to be cheerful, and her pale face was kind and beautiful.

She had one friend, the boy who looked after the geese. Often he played on his pipe to cheer her, and Tattercoats danced to the music, while the geese waddled after her with outstretched necks and flapping wings. Then she and the goose-boy would laugh until they had to stop.

One day a messenger on a fine horse reined up at the castle gates.

"The king commands your presence at a great ball," he proclaimed, "to celebrate his son's coming of age. On that night the prince will choose his bride."

Not for years had there been such a stir! The old man summoned the barber to cut his beard, the laundry maid to wash his linen, and the tailor to make him new clothes.

Tattercoats begged to go with him.

"What! A scarecrow like you?" scolded her grandfather. "Get back to the kitchen where you belong."

Off he went, while poor Tattercoats sat down in the courtyard and for once gave way to tears.

"Never mind, Tattercoats," comforted the goose-boy. "We'll still have some fun. We'll walk to the palace together and watch all the fine people as they arrive. And we'll see the fireworks at night. There are sure to be fireworks!"

So Tattercoats cheered up at once like the brave girl that she was, and they set out together. The goose-boy played his pipe, and Tattercoats danced along the road beside him, while the geese flapped and followed in solemn procession, two by two.

Soon they heard hoof-beats behind them. A young man overtook them – a very handsome young man, richly dressed. He looked at the geese and laughed. Then he looked at Tattercoats and swung down from his horse.

"We are going the same way," he said. "Let us travel together."

He was so good a companion that soon they were talking like old friends. He loved Tattercoats for her beauty and gentleness, and she loved him for his kindness.

"Tattercoats," he said at last, "will you marry me?"

Tattercoats' eyes filled with tears.

"No," she said. "A poor ragged girl is no fit bride for a great lord like you."

Try as he would, he could not persuade her.

"Then promise me just one thing," he said. "Come to the hall of the palace at midnight, that I may see you at least once more."

Tattercoats promised, and the young man rode on into the palace courtyard.

Midnight came, the time when the prince must choose his bride.

As everyone waited for him to speak, the doors of the hall swung wide, and in came Tattercoats and the goose-boy, with all the geese flapping behind them two by two. The astonished lords and ladies laughed till the tears ran down their cheeks.

But the prince stepped down from his throne and went straight to Tattercoats. He took her hands and kissed them.

"This," he said, "is my chosen bride. I will marry no other."

At that very moment Tattercoats' rags fell away, and she stood before them all radiant in a gown of softest gold.

Just behind her, glowing with joy for his friend's happiness, the goose-boy had grown into a tall and handsome squire clad in rich blue velvet and silver. And, where the geese had been, two rows of splendid pages in white and gold held up the train of Tattercoats' dress.

The prince and Tattercoats were married the very next day. As for the old, cold, grey grandfather, he had laughed with everyone else. And the laughter blew away his gloom. He went back to his castle and opened all the windows, so that the wind blew away the cobwebs and the sun shone in and he could hear the ring of birdsong in the world outside.

Slowly he forgot his sulks and became what all good grandfathers should be. And when Tattercoats' children came to play, the castle was as happy as the palace itself.

MORE PICTURE BOOKS IN PAPERBACK FROM FRANCES LINCOLN

LITTLE INCHKIN

Fiona French

Little Inchkin is only as big as a lotus flower, but he has the courage of a Samurai warrior. How he proves his valour, wins the hand of a princess, and is granted his dearest wish by the Lord Buddha is charmingly retold in this Tom Thumb legend of old Japan.

Suitable for National Curriculum English - Reading, Key Stages 1 and 2
Scottish Guidelines, English Language - Reading, Levels A and B

ISBN 0-7112-0917-0 £4.99

CHINYE

Obi Onyefulu
Illustrated by Evie Safarewicz

Poor Chinye! Back and forth through the forest she goes, fetching and carrying for her cruel stepmother. But strange powers are watching over her, and soon her life will be magically transformed... An enchanting retelling of a traditional West African folk tale of goodness, greed and a treasure-house of gold.

Suitable for National Curriculum English - Reading, Key Stages 1 and 2
Scottish Guidelines, English Language - Reading, Level B

ISBN 0-7112-1052-7 £4.99

CINDERELLA AND THE HOT AIR BALLOON

Ann Jungman
Illustrated by Russell Ayto

Go to the boring old ball? Cinderella would far rather throw her own party. And when Prince Charming turns up, they find they have some rather unexpected tastes in common... A hilarious new version of the well-known fairy story that every child will love.

Suitable for National Curriculum English - Reading, Key Stages 1 and 2
Scottish Guidelines, English Language - Reading, Levels A and B

ISBN 0-7112-1051-9 £4.99

All Frances Lincoln titles are available at your local bookshop or by post from:
Frances Lincoln Books, B.B.C.S., P.O. Box 941, Hull, North Humberside, HU1 3YQ.
24 Hour Credit Card Line 01482 224626
To order, send:
Title, author, ISBN number and price for each book ordered.
Your full name and address.
Cheque or postal order made payable to B.B.C.S.
for the total amount, plus postage and packing as below.
U.K. & B.F.P.O. - £1.00 for the first book,
and 50p for each additional book up to a maximum of £3.50.
Overseas & Eire - £2.00 for the first book, £1.00 for the second
and 50p for each additional book.

Prices and availability are subject to change without notice.